The Book, the Vow and the Blade

by   Crystal Nolen

Wider Perspectives Publishing   ∞   2024   ∞   Hampton Roads, Va.

The Book
The Vow
and
The Blade

Cover Photography by Andre (Dray) Washington

Copyright ©2024 Crystal Nolen 1-13324058001 verified, TXu2-407-102 Crystal Nolen
1st run release Sept. 2024, Hampton Roads, Va
ISBN: 978-1-964531-21-2

Dedication

This story is humbly dedicated to the Creator of Life, and my
Mother and Father for bringing me into existence… my
Ancestors – both new and long crossed-over for their ever
present, inspirational perseverance… and my Family and
Friends… for their love and support.

Contents

*Ecclesiastes 1:11 ~ There is no remembrance
of former things; neither shall there be any remembrance
of things to come with those that shall come after.*

2014

Officers investigated an early morning crime scene in Suffolk County's Presidential Building. "Come on, people, let's get everything fingerprinted and DNA'd up. Officer Boykin has the perimeter team in place. This building is officially locked down until further notice," commanded Detective Stanley Parker.

Detective Parker knelt to look into the dead man's face. He stood and straightened his Pittsburgh Steelers cap. His youthful physique was evident beneath his worn T-shirt and jeans.

Detective Jones covered his nose to keep out the thick haze of marijuana smoke that permeated throughout the space of the luxuriously decorated apartment.

Next to an unfinished glass of wine, a line of cocaine stretched across a gold-framed mirror on the edge of the garden tub. The chanting of a ritual song played from the surround sound stereo system while detectives and officers searched the apartment, taking pictures and logging information.

Detective Jones entered the bathroom.

Detective Parker asked, "Where's Frank?"

Jones replied, "Oh, you wanted me to call him?"

"What do you think 'call Bryant' means?"

The repeating rhythm of the song pulsating through the crime scene shocks Detective Jones's system. "I can't think. Can somebody please turn that damn jungle music down? It's hypnotizing me!"

Parker glared at him. "Nobody touch a damn thing in here till we get prints! You probably need to be hypnotized. It might help you."

Jones fumbled with his cell phone. It fell on the floor next to the victim's decapitated head.

Parker became even more agitated.

Jones picked up the phone and went into the hallway to call Detective Bryant. The shaken detective rejoined the others inside, dusting for fingerprints. Finally, the chanting stopped, and Jones regained his composure.

Frank Bryant strolled in and stepped into the bathroom with Parker. "Sorry, Parker, I was at the church."

"He gave his only begotten son that whosoever believeth in him shall not perish but have everlasting life. That's what it says, right?" recited Parker.

"John 3:16. That's the scripture," Bryant replied while kneeling to get a better look. "This is Chaplain Caldena?"

"Yep. From bath to beheading. This is a fine example of the cruelty of human beings and, from that, the need to believe in a life other than this one." Parker shook his head.

Bryant moved in for a closer inspection of the illegal layout. "You think this was staged?"

"Could be. We'll start with a toxicology report and go from there."

The detectives stepped out of the bathroom and into the master suite. Parker pointed to a prescription bottle on the bed.

Bryant pulled a handkerchief from his pocket and picked up the bottle. He read aloud, "Prescribed to Mauritzio Caldena by Dr. George McKay...Lithium..."

"Lithium? Serious mind-altering stuff there. How many pills left?" queried the senior detective.

"It's empty," answered Bryant.

Parker replied with a deep sigh while walking around the dead man's bedroom. "Have you heard the joke about the chaplain and the psychiatrist?"

"No," replied Bryant.

Parker started, "A chaplain and a psychiatrist walk into a bar. They sit down next to a lawyer and start talking over a few rounds of drinks."

Bryant waited. "And, what happened?"

"Confessions, therapy, legal advice – I can't tell you what they talked about. It's all confidential, but the bartender got a book deal out of it."

Bryant chuckled and continued to followed Parker.

The sun shone through the panoramic glass, warming the sleek, modern décor of the horrific scene. Parker was thinking in reverse as he returned to the front entrance to examine the door again. "No forced entry," he stated. He eyed Bryant, "Is that another new suit?"

Parker was deep into his investigation process — a barrage of observations mixed with random thoughts. He called it dancing, and Bryant was a quick study with a nimble step.

"Clean cut. Little splatter. Most of the blood is in the tub… Oh, I got it! You're in love," stated Parker.

"I am in love with life. No water on the floor, no struggle, no murder weapon," Bryant chimed back.

"Make sure you notify the next of kin," Parker added, "so, what's her name?"

"What are you talking about, old man?" Bryant quipped.

"You know what I am talking about. Who's the lady you're wearing those new suits for?" replied Parker.

"Can't a brother upgrade his wardrobe? I plead the fifth. Who made the call?" Bryant tried to dodge Parker's focus on his love life.

"The maid found him. Her supervisor made the call," Parker replied.

"You would think an upscale place like this would have plenty of security," wondered Bryant.

"Only a doorman and three security cameras. One at the main entrance, one in the rear at the loading docks, and one in the lounge," responded Parker.

"So, let's assume — " began Bryant.

Parker interrupted him. "Remember my motto?" The younger detective replied, "Yes, don't assume anything."

Parker shook his head, and Bryant corrected himself, "Don't assume shit because you might miss shit."

Parker smiled, "That's better." Stepping onto the victim's balcony, Parker watched the grounds below. He pulled out an electronic cigarette and puffed to inhale its vapor. "This is bad."

"I know, Chaplain Caldena was scheduled to officiate the Centennial Celebration. The opening parade is today," said Bryant.

Parker corrected him, "No, I'm talking about this digital cigarette. It ain't worth a damn!" He pulled out a fresh pack of Newport cigarettes, opened it, and lit one. He slid the clear wrapper tab in his pocket, careful not to contaminate the crime scene.

"Did you go to your meeting yesterday?" asked Bryant.

"A man's head has been chopped off, and you want to know if I went to a meeting?" Parker asked. Parker took a drag from his cigarette. He explained, "Those meetings, man, everybody's huddled around waiting to tell their sad stories, and waiting to hear my sad story and the things I have seen. No disrespect to anyone, but those meetings aren't for me."

"I know what you've told me, and I can't imagine going through that. I want to make sure you're alright," he assured Parker.

Parker replied, "Sometimes it seems like I have lived several lifetimes, each filled with so much pain. But we all have crosses to bear, so don't worry about me."

Bryant moved in next to him. "Come on, Stan, you're like a father to me. You're the closest thing I have to family."
Parker stared out across the landscape. "To tell you the truth, listening to people talk about how much they used to drink and do drugs makes me want to drink and do drugs again."

They laughed.

Parker turned to Bryant. "I can do this better by myself. You know what I mean?"

"I know what you mean, but you know I'm here if you need me," reassured Bryant.

"I know. You'd better be worried about getting a partner as good as me when I'm gone."

"You have been retiring for the last – how many years?" Bryant recalled.

"No, don't take this for a joke, son," he added, "I'm serious this time." He put the cigarette out and shoved the butt in his pocket, again careful not to contaminate the crime scene. "This is the last dance for me." Parker turned to go back inside.

Bryant followed him.

"Remember, I need you to —"

Bryant's cell phone rang, interrupting Parker. "I got it – the next of kin. I need to answer this call. I'll meet you back at the station."

Bryant headed toward the elevators, and Parker returned to the master suite for another look. He felt like he was missing something. He got down on his hands and knees to look beneath the bed. Something shiny grabbed his attention, and he called an officer into the bedroom to bag the evidence found under the bed.

1906

Like a wet quilt, thick humidity laid over Montvane Estate. Buzzing with mosquitos and fireflies, the evening sky began to dim.

Little Lizzie hid behind the bushes on the side of the barn. She looked through a small gap between two slats of wood. The ten-year-old girl could see men in hooded robes greeting each other with strange handshakes.

George Montvane secured the barn doors. He lit a row of candles in the center of the barn.

The seven hooded figures chanted and circled the flames.

George Junior smiled as he handed his father the shiny sword. One of the men untied the tiny boy's hands.

Lizzie recognized the little boy, Ben, whose family lived at the bottom of the hill.

The man shoved little Ben into the center of the circle. The chanting grew louder as George Senior waved the sword back and forth in front of the boy's eyes. Paralyzed with fear, the boy lay on his stomach across a wooden stump.

George Senior raised the blade and swiped down through the boy's neck. His head rolled onto the dusty barn floor.

Lizzie was frozen. She could not pull herself away from the fear locked into little Ben's dead eyes.

A crow screamed from a tree above Lizzie's head rousing her from shock. She ran home as fast as she could as evening turned into night around her.

Daylight shone brightly as Lizzie navigated the truck toward Main Street. "I forgot about this damned parade!" she complained aloud to herself. Lizzie rearranged a picture of Ben and Aunt Sassie on the truck's console as she waited for the parade to pass.

A colorful collection of floats and battalions made up the processional march of bands in colonial regalia playing patriotic anthems to celebrate the sovereignty of the County. The hot, humid air seemed to melt the vibrant costumes into a collage of waving figures.

Lizzie rubbed her aching stomach. Beads of sweat rolled down her face and back. She turned up the air conditioning and sipped from her water bottle. "What is wrong with me? Lord, please have mercy on my soul," she prayed out loud, "and let this be the end of this parade."

Six men in black hooded robes riding big, black horses brought up the rear of the parade. The last man in the group guided a white horse with no rider. The white horse looked familiar to her, and just as she realized whose horse it was, her phone rang.

"I'm stuck in this parade traffic. My stomach feels horrible. It has been aching all day. No. I don't want to go to a doctor. I just want to get home and get back into bed. I'll be fine. I don't want to do anything. It's no big deal. I will have other birthdays, but I do need to see you."

She felt nauseous and rolled down the windows to let in some fresh air. A truckload of teenagers followed the parade, waving a Confederate flag, rebel-yelling, and blaring the truck's horn.

"Wait, I can't hear you," she paused her conversation.

One of the juveniles threw a bottle in Lizzie's direction, and it shattered a few feet away from her truck. She was in too much pain to respond to the foolery.

"I'm okay. It's just some kids riding by. You know how wild they can get around here. And with the Centennial, God only knows how crazy it will get this week."

The parade cleared, and she maneuvered her green pickup truck across Main Street. Her phone beeped, "I've got another call."

Lizzie switched lines to answer the call from a private number. "Hello." She could hear someone breathing. "Hello? Who is this?" The breathing sounded familiar. "George, is that you? Can you hear me?"

The call disconnected, and the phone rang again with a number she didn't recognize.

"Hello?"

"Hello. This is Detective Stanley Parker with the County PD."

The click of Lizzie's high heels on the marble floor echoed down the hallway of the police station. A door opened.

"Elizabeth?"

"Detective Parker?"

He shook her hand and led her into an interrogation room.

"This is Detective Bryant and Detective Jones." Bryant shook her hand.

"What is this about?"

"Do you know Chaplain Caldena?" Parker asked.

"Yes, I do," Lizzie replied.

"He's dead," added Parker.

"What happened?" Lizzie asked.

"You tell us. We know the two of you met yesterday. Right?" Detective Jones asked

"Yes. I met him for lunch."

The Detective replied, "The chaplain was found dead this morning in his apartment at the Presidential, and we know what goes on up on that hill! Was he one of your tricks?"

Jones was an easy read for her. His shoulders were heavy with the pain and rejection of his life. His attempt to become a special agent was evidenced by the old Bureau Academy lanyard he wore around his neck everyday since his failing their compentency evaluation. Abused by his mother, his childhood pain had brewed into a poisonous attitude towards women. He asked, "Well, how do you know him?"

She straightened her back, ready for his next attack.

"He and my Aunt Sassie were on the County Advisory Board and worked on several development projects together. Why are you asking me these questions?"

"You were the last person to see Chaplain Caldena alive."

She shook her head. "If I were the last person to see him alive, then I'd be the killer. And the story would be over."

He imagined himself alone with her. "You're a sassy one, huh? I know what to do with you. We could keep you right here, in the County lockup!"

Lizzie responded, "So you're going to arrest me for eating a club sandwich with him?" She looked at Detective Bryant. "I told you we had lunch, and I left him in the lounge."

Detective Parker asked, "How well do you know the chaplain?"

"Well, enough for him to invite me to lunch to advise me on my aunt's affairs."

Parker added, "Have you ever been inside the chaplain's apartment?"

Lizzie responded. "Yes, several times."

"Maybe to have a glass of wine, do a little coke, a little bump and grind? That's what you people call it, right?" Jones was probing for a nefarious connection that could feed his prejudice.

She stood to leave. "You see, Detective Jones, you don't know who you're talking to. So, let me get to the root of your problem. I'm sorry that your mother left you locked in that closet all those times to hear her and all those men doing those ungodly things. I am so sorry that she was not a good mother to you. Maybe you should look into getting some counseling. We all have crosses to bear, but I'm not your mother."

Jones replied, "Go to hell! I can get a magistrate's order to hold you in custody right now!"

Parker and Bryant stood.

Parker stated, "That won't be necessary." Then he addressed the woman, "If we have any more questions, we'll be in touch."

Suddenly, she doubled over in pain, holding her stomach.

Parker and Bryant rushed to help her. "Are you okay? Should we call a doctor?"

"No. I am fine," she responded.

"You don't look well. Let me help you."

Bryant returned after helping Lizzie to her car.

"You're the nicest guy I know escorting murder suspects to their cars," quipped Jones.

"She's not a suspect," responded Bryant.

"He's a real gentleman. You should take notes," remarked Parker.

Jones adjusts the Bureau Academy lanyard around his neck, "She's our perp. I know it."

"Case closed, huh?" Bryant sighed.

"Seen her kind before. She knows too much for her own damn good. A high-class whore that needs a good hard fuck!" he proclaimed.

"You need to check yourself. You already crossed the line. Have some respect for the lady," Bryant added.

"You're supposed to be the expert. What do you think, Parker?" Jones asked.

"Too soon to tell," said Parker.

2014

Dusk turned to night and beat Lizzie home once again. She opened the front door, entered the kitchen, and set her bag down on the counter.

"Hands up, Happy Birthday!" Ben shouted as he jumped out from behind the door.

"What the hell are you doing?" she asked.

"You said no more guns," answered Ben.

"That's right. No more guns," shaking her head.

Ben reminds her, "But I'm older than you."

Lizzie added, "Ben, you know how much I hate guns!"

He placed the toy gun in her hand. Then he reached into his belt and pulled out a plastic dagger. She followed him into the living room.

She asked, "Is she here yet?"

"No," Ben answered.

"Has she called?" she inquired again.

"No. What's the matter with you?" He added," You look sick."

Lizzie replied, "I'll be alright."

He paused the movie and kissed her cheek. "It was hot today, but I mowed the whole east lawn. Tomorrow, I'll trim the rose bushes by the guesthouse. When are they going to deliver the wood for me to fix the fence?"

Lizzie flipped through a few pieces of mail.

Ben resumed the movie. It was his favorite, and he knew every scene. He jumped up from his seat, mimicking the action on the screen. "This my favorite part!" He sliced through the air with his toy weapon.

"I think they're going to deliver it tomorrow. Make sure they come through the back gate and offload the wood behind the barn. The last time, they almost ruined the heather shrubs."

He did not respond. He was lost in the movie.

She checked to see if there were any missed calls on her cell phone. "Aunt Sassie would have a fit if she knew they rode over her heather."

Ben mutes the volume. "She did have a fit! They were unloading, and out of nowhere, the door they'd propped open just loosed itself and smacked the driver so hard on the backside that half the hill heard it. Aunt Sassie got him good."

They laughed. "It's the truth. She's still here with us. You can't feel her? You can't see her?"

"I haven't been myself lately."

"You need to go to the doctor?" he asked.

"No. I hate doctors." She began to cry. She tried to hold back the tears.

Ben wrapped her in his arms. "Don't cry. It'll be okay, Lizzie. You'll see her again, just like I do. You're sad, that's all. When you get happy again, you'll be able to see everything just like before, okay? I'll take care of you, sis."

"I don't know what I'd do without you, Ben."

"I cooked meatloaf, mashed potatoes, green beans, and rolls for your birthday. I made your plate. It's in the microwave. Want me to heat it up for you?"

"That sounds good. I'm going to take a bath first."

"Okay. I'll bring it upstairs when you get out the tub." Ben resumed his knife wielding re-enactment.

A few minutes later, upstairs in her bedroom, Lizzie slipped off her shoes and turned on the television. She went into the bathroom and turned on the faucet to fill the tub. While waiting, she stared at a picture on her dresser of Aunt Sassie, Olivia, Ben, and her that was taken on the front porch years ago. She picked up the picture and touched Aunt Sassie's face.

"I miss you so much."

1985

In the setting sun, Sassie's house, a two-story colonial-style home adorned with magnolia trees and heather shrubs and nestled in thick green grass, stood like a fortress.

Perched up on the top of the hill, the wrap-around porch provided beautiful views of the County from all sides.

A social worker brought Lizzie, six years old, to Sassie Walker's door.

The social worker left the girl with the woman with the long, black braids.

The woman motioned for the girl to put down her bag and to follow her into the kitchen. "Come on back here with me, baby. I got a pot of chicken and dumplings on the stove."

The woman gave the girl's hand a gentle tug. The girl did not move. "Don't you want some chicken and dumplings?"

Streams of tears rolled down the girl's cheeks. "I wanna go home with my family," she cried.

Sassie never knew her family. Her mother died while giving birth to her two months early. All her life, she had been told how her mother had proclaimed a special prophecy over the child growing insider of her. She had also heard how she resembled the Constance family of Suffolk County. After her husband died, she came to the County to find out if the rumors were true.

They were. Her birth records told the story of her Mulatto father and her Native American mother. With her lineage documented and her inheritance secured, she decided to stay in the

County and wait to see what life would bring her way, and to see her mother's prophecy fully revealed.

Sassie gently pulled the girl close trying to console her. The girl began to calm down in Sassie's embrace, her stifled cry still heaving in her chest and jumping in her throat.

Sassie prayed, "Creator of all life, please protect this baby, and give her strength and peace."

Looking into the crying girl's eyes, Sassie could see the prophecy coming to life. She knew she would need to train this special girl for the battles she must fight. It was her duty to prepare this child for what was to come.

The pigtailed girl looked around the woman, and her teary eyes ascended the beautiful staircase. Her little body was weighed down with sadness, but her spirit felt safe in this house with the old woman.

2014

After her bath, Lizzie devoured the plate of food Ben brought upstairs for her. She stretched across the bed, eventually falling to sleep. A strange noise roused her. By the time she spotted the figure in the mirror, it was too late.

Taken to one of the Bureau's top-secret underground interrogation rooms, she focused on the dark figures standing around her. She struggled to stand, but the cold, magnetic bands on her wrists and ankles paralyzed her.

"We are watching you," warned one of the figures in the room.

Another added, "You had better stay in your place."

Lizzie replied, "I was in my place. At home in my bedroom. Just a few minutes ago. Why am I being called in like this?"

"Your orders were to stand down," added the third figure.

"But the mission is not complete," replied Lizzie.

"The mission has been suspended," one of the figures replied.

"It can't be," she demanded.

The second figure asked, "Do you know how much you stand to lose disobeying a direct order?"

"I know how much I stand to gain," Lizzie answered.

The third figure declared, "This is not how it's supposed to be. The chaplain should not have been first."

Lizzie reminded them, "This is the true order. Only a few people have ever seen the book. Aunt Sassie studied the book. And you know where she put it? In my head! It was written this way! The chaplain had to be sacrificed first to break the seal. None of you know the true secret of the Centennial, but I do...and he does."

"Your orders are to stand down!" declared the second figure.

"I have been called to duty by one higher than all of you, and I will not stand down!"

2014

Lizzie was returned to her home and dozed off before sunrise. Someone knocked at her bedroom door.

"Come in," she called out.

Olivia opened the bedroom door and switched on the light. "Hey sleepy head?"

"Hey, I thought you'd be here yesterday?" asked Lizzie

"A 'how you doing' would be nice."

"A 'happy birthday' would have been nice, too."

"Happy birthday, sis! I'm sorry I missed it." She reached down and kissed Lizzie's forehead.

"Where are your bags?" Lizzie asked.

"At the hotel," Olivia responded.

"The hotel? Why would you get a hotel?" Lizzie was puzzled.

"No reason. Just in case I need to get away."

"Get away from what, Olivia?"

Olivia walked across the room to look out of the window. A young girl sat alone at the bottom of the hill, waiting for the first bus of the day.

"The memories... I didn't realize how long it's been. How much I missed you, Ben, Aunt Sassie and this house."

Lizzie sank back beneath the covers with a sigh.

"You must hate me?" asked Olivia.

"Don't say that. I love you. You're my sister. I just haven't been myself lately."

"What's wrong?"

Lizzie rolled over. "I'll tell you about it later. I'm going back to sleep."

Olivia turned out the light and slid into the bed next to Lizzie. She fell asleep thinking about the young girl waiting at the bus stop.

1991

A 12-year-old girl sat on the bench at the bus stop at sunrise. After watching the girl from the window, Lizzie grabbed her sweater and went outside and down to the bottom of the hill.

"The bus doesn't stop here anymore," Lizzie told the girl.

"I'm not waiting on the bus. My mother meets me here," the girl answered quickly.

Lizzie sat down next to her. "Why aren't you in school?"

Olivia responded, "Why you not in school?"

"I am. Aunt Sassie is my teacher. She teaches me way more than regular school. You're 12, like me. Your favorite color is yellow. And your momma's name is Eileen."

"How do you know that?" Olivia was confused.

"I just know. Aunt Sassie does, too." Lizzie slid closer to Olivia.

"My momma died. My brother, too. They say I can't live with my daddy. So that's why I live here. Aunt Sassie's not my real aunt, but she treats me like her child." She turned toward the girl and touched her stringy, blonde hair.

"You can stay with us."

"What about my mother?"

"She's… She can't meet you anymore."

Olivia's anticipation was extinguished with sadness and fear.

"It's safe here. Aunt Sassie will protect you. He can't hurt you if you stay here with us." Lizzie stood and headed back up the hill. Olivia followed.

2014

It was morning, and Olivia was cooking breakfast. The smell of fried potatoes and onions floated through the house, along with the morning sunshine.

The doorbell rang. Lizzie answered the door. "Good morning, gentlemen. Come in."

The detectives stepped into the foyer. Lizzie led them into the main sitting room. Olivia and Ben entered from the kitchen.

"Good morning," Olivia greeted the men, "I didn't know we had guests."

Lizzie introduced the men, "This is Detective Parker and Detective Bryant."

Ben took a seat on the couch, quietly watching the two men.

Olivia wiped her hands on her apron before shaking their hands. "Would you gentlemen like some breakfast?"

"I'm sure this is not a social call," chimed Lizzie.

"No, it's not. But thank you," Detective Bryant replied.

Parker announced, "There's been another murder at the Presidential." he added, "The body of Attorney General Frattini was found this morning."

Lizzie was silent.

"You mind coming back down to the station to answer a few more questions?" requested Parker.

"Questions, for what? My sister wouldn't hurt a fly," interrupted Olivia.

"Your sister?" Detective Bryant looked surprised.

"Yep, me, the White kid, her and Ben, the Black kids raised right here in this house together, by a Blackfoot Indian woman. A real Rainbow Coalition," described Olivia.

Detective Bryant responded with a smile, "It is a pleasure to meet you."

"I would say the same, but under the circumstances, I am not so sure," she smiled back.

"So, Elizabeth, we'll see you down at the station?" asked Detective Parker.

Lizzie nodded, then walked the men to the door. Ben watched from the window as they pulled away from the curb.

2014

Inside the County Police Headquarters, Agent Carolyn Brown reviewed the interrogation video conducted earlier that day with the three detectives.

Detective Jones asked, "She's lying, right?"

"Concealing." answered Agent Brown

"She knows something about the murder, doesn't she?" Jones pressed, especially curious.

"It's complicated," replied Agent Brown.

Lizzie's voice filled the room, as the video continued to play, "His mother left when he was six. She could sing like a bird, and one day, she just flew away and never came back. Ben and his father lived down the road. Aunt Sassie adored them. After Ben's father died, that was it. Ben had no other family. The County tried to take his house and put him into an institution. Aunt Sassie fought the County and became his guardian. Before she passed, I promised her that we would stay together, like blood, and help each other." Lizzie smiled.

She remembered how Ben's father was so caring and tender with him. Raised him to love himself and overcome the things that the doctors said would limit his potential. Ben's father never listened to any of the doctors when it came to that. He raised Ben to be a strong, hardworking, and loving individual.

Agent Brown added, "She and Ben have a strong bond." The video continued, "He is autistic, and he's amazing in so many ways. He takes care of the house, he helped take care of Aunt

Sassie and he tries to take care of me. He cooks, cleans, and handles whatever needs to be done on the property."

Agent Brown looked at Detective Parker. "What do you think?"

"About Ben? Oh, he's a big teddy bear," Parker replied.

"A big, crazy, black bear. He's got a charge for resisting arrest," Jones declared.

"According to the report, he got into a scuffle with a mental health counselor years ago, right after his father died," added Bryant.

"What about the sister?" queried Agent Brown.

Detective Bryant explained, "Her mother was found dead when she was 12. People think it was the father, but he was never charged. The sister left years ago. She's been living in Texas. She's had a couple of serious possession charges, and she's been in rehab a few times."

Detective Jones wondered, "But why is she here now?"

Bryant answered, "To help with family business, maybe?"

Detective Jones added, "Or to see if she can get more money for drugs, huh?"

"Go back to the question about the ex-husband," Agent Brown directed. Jones found the spot and played the video. On the screen, Lizzie shifted in her chair. Her lean, delicate frame elongated like a gazelle poised to sprint. They continued to watch the interrogation.

Jones asked, "When was the last time you saw him?"

Agent Brown motioned toward the video screen. "Watch her body language. She becomes protective. She's afraid for him. She feels the need to protect him."

The interrogation video continued to play, and Jones' voice flowed from the recording. "That's a lie! You told us you hadn't spoken to him since the funeral!"

Lizzie responded, "Sending someone papers in the mail is not speaking to them. What does my ex-husband have to do with this anyway?"

Brown motioned for Jones to stop the video.

Jones was burning to know, "How long has she been with the Bureau?"

"That's classified," responded Agent Brown as she closed her briefcase and slipped on her jacket.

Detective Parker asked, "What's her status?"

"Medical hold."

"For what?" Jones asked.

She smiled. "That's classified. Parker will update you, per my report, on a need-to-know basis. Have a good evening."

Parker walked Brown to the elevator where she offered, "Off the record, I can tell you she has special skills, special senses. She was the first female on Seal Team Six, and even though the Bureau hasn't acknowledged her publicly, she's done very important work for us."

Parker wondered, "Is she a loose cannon?"

"Doesn't matter. If this gets out, the public will think we've lost control."

"Brings back bad memories," added Parker.

She slides her arm under his. "How long has it been, Stan?"

"Let's see, I think the last time I saw you was in the hallway at the Bureau right before they canned my ass."

"Has it been that long?"

"Sometimes it seems like lifetimes ago, and then other times it seems like just yesterday."

"You sure are looking great."

"Got to stay in shape. Turn a few heads, you know, I'm still sexy." They laughed together.

"You know what the old folks around here used to say would happen on the Centennial?" added Agent Brown.

"Don't tell me things have got that damn bad up at the Bureau. Old wives' tales about demons in hooded robes is not evidence."

"Well, we wrestle not against flesh and blood but against spiritual wickedness in high places. It's something to think about."

The elevator arrived. "So, what are you going to tell your husband?"

"Agent Connor will get my full report and recommendation tonight."

1991

The midday sun showered its attention on the glorious house while wrapping it in a shining aura of protection.

Aunt Sassie raised her reading glasses and reached for the photo. Olivia's father stood at the door like a snake, ready to strike. His new wife trembled, waiting for the older woman to respond.

"Oh yes, I've seen this child. I saw her sitting at the bus stop down the hill."

Sassie asked, "How long you say you been looking for her?"

The woman answered, "We ain't seen Olivia in five months. He thought it would be a good idea to lay low down in Louisville at my folk's place."

"Shut up! She was talking to me," the man responded. "Yeah, it's been a while since we've seen her. You got a real nice place here." Olivia's father tried to step inside. Sassie swelled up and filled the doorway.

Knowing how easy it could be for him to lose control, the woman grabbed her husband's arm. "Come on, honey, let's go."

"Just wait a fucking minute! If she's in there, she's coming with me!"

"Honey, please watch your temper." the woman replied.

"I tell you what, if my kid's in there–."

Aunt Sassie querried, "You say you haven't seen her in five months?"

"Look, lady, I don't want no trouble with you. I'm just trying to find the kid and make sure we get what belongs to her."

"Yeah, her mother died and left her some insurance money. We're moving to the big city, right baby?" the woman smiled brightly.

"You stupid broad! If there ain't no kid, there ain't no money!" he said to the woman.

The man heard movement inside the house at the top of the stairs. "If that little heifer is in there, you'd better send her out! Tell her she better get her ass out here right now! Her daddy is here." The man grew agitated and loud. He began to yell at the top of his lungs. "I'm sorry, baby, I'll never hurt you again. We'll have a brand-new life, just come out here before I fuckin' lose it!" He stared at Sassie, wishing he could move her with his eyes. But he couldn't. He added, "And she knows got-damn it! She knows how it gets when I lose it!"

The two girls drew back deeper into the darkness concealing them at the top of the staircase.

Aunt Sassie had a plan. She picked up the phone from the table next to the door.

"The police been looking for your little girl. They said if anyone came asking about her to call them." Sassie picked up the phone with one hand and fingered the handle of the dagger in her apron with the other hand.

The man took a step back.

"Hello, yes, I'm calling about the missing girl. A detective said to call if anyone came around asking about her. Yes, her father and stepmother are here. They say she ran away, and they haven't seen her in five months. Okay, yes, uh-huh, that will be good." She looked toward the man, "They say they gonna send an officer from the precinct around the corner, but they want to speak to you," she extends the phone's receiver.

The man rejected the phone, "I think this might be the wrong house. Honey, come on. Can't you walk any fuckin' faster? Let's get the hell out of here!"

The words "police" and "probation" hung in the air as they jumped in the car and speed away.

Aunt Sassie knew that the couple would not return anytime soon. She placed the phone back in its cradle; it had been disconnected for weeks.

As far as Sassie was concerned, it was official, Olivia had found a safe place to call home.

2014

As the long day morphed into a night, Olivia lit an incense and poured herself another double shot of whiskey while her favorite CD played. She poured a shot for Lizzie.

Lizzie walked through the living room headed upstairs.

Olivia, drink in hand, watched her. "Have a drink with me."

"No whiskey. I'll take a ginger ale."

"You need to relax. I'll run you a hot bath." Olivia's phone rang. She silenced it.

Lizzie assured her, "I'm fine. Don't forget Mr. Levine will be coming in the morning."

Olivia went to the bar and poured Lizzie a ginger ale. "You've changed... you seem so cold. Like a machine."

"Thanks."

"I'm not trying to hurt your feelings. I'm just telling you the truth."

Lizzie looked away. Olivia had been gone for a long time. It seemed too late to pick up where they left off, and now, they both were keeping secrets.

"Things are just not the same. Sometimes, I don't know what the truth is or who's telling it."

"Love is the truth," replied Olivia.

Olivia sat on the couch next to Lizzie.

Olivia sipped her drink. She reached for a half-smoked joint perched in the ashtray. She relit it and tried to pass it to Lizzie, but Lizzie shook her head.

"You're not smoking with me?"

"No, I haven't done that in years."

"I guess I take after Aunt Sassie. You remember she always kept bags of herbs with her." They laughed.

"Those were different herbs."

"It's all from the Earth, c'mon Lizzie, have a puff, it'll be like old times. It'll settle your stomach."

"No. Where's Ben?"

"In bed. He's upset about Mr. Levine coming over tomorrow."

Olivia took another toke.

"Why, what's wrong?"

"I thought you knew everything. You mean there's something you don't know?" Olivia was amused.

"Seriously, Olivia, what's wrong with Ben?"

"He thought Mr. Levine was coming because the County was going to take him away."

"Lord have mercy, I'll go talk to him."

"I handled it. He's fine now." Olivia took another puff and exhaled the smoke after a few seconds.

"So, what did you say? What did you tell him?"

"You don't trust me to explain something to Ben?"

"Maybe I do. Maybe I don't. That depends on just what you said."

"I told him Mr. Levine was coming for us to sign some papers for Aunt Sassie and, since you must know, I also told him that you would never let anything happen to him or me. Was that a good enough explanation for you?" She paused. "I've been thinking about moving back to the County, but things are complicated."

"Complicated. What do you mean?" Lizzie replied. "There's nothing that can't be fixed, one way or another."

"There *is* something..." Olivia looked away as her eyes welled up with tears.

"You're not going to cry, are you? You're going to ruin your high. Try to be happy and think of the good times."

"I'm okay. I love you, that's all. I want you to know I love you, and I am sorry."

"Sorry for what, Olivia?"

"For not being here."

"No, I'm sorry. I used to envy you because you had a daddy to go to. My mom and brother were – well, you know, and I couldn't see my dad. All I had was you, Aunt Sassie, and Ben," Lizzie revealed.

"Do you forgive me for not being here when she passed?" Olivia asked.

"Yes, I forgive you. Do you forgive me for being jealous of you?" Lizzie asked.

Olivia stood. "Yes, of course, I forgive you. But, Lizzie, it was terrible when I went back with my dad. I missed you, Ben, and Aunt Sassie so much. It feels good to be home where I should have stayed. I was chasing a love that never existed."

Wiping away her tears, she reached for Lizzie, and they waltzed around the room. She hummed the tune to their special song.

They recalled the day, not long after they met at the bus stop, when they pricked blood from their fingers, mashed them together, and made up the verses to their blood sister song – singing together, "Like a flower that busies the bee. Like the air all around, we can't see. Bonded by blood, eternally. Sisters forever, you and me."

Olivia and Lizzie danced around the room giggling like little girls before their embrace ended. "I'm going to get your bath ready."

After Olivia left the room, Lizzie pulled up her blouse and stared at the rapidly increasing bulge in her abdomen. She feared that what was growing inside her was draining her special senses. Lizzie had never been sick. Olivia was the child who had needed attention for colds, ear infections, and strep throat. A slight breeze against her pale, white skin would put her in bed for days. Lizzie was the child who would slip out at night to dance in the rain and snow of a winter storm with not as much as a sniffle the next day. The men in the units she worked with were always amazed at her stamina. And her ability to withstand extreme pain and pack trauma away in the blink of an eye. She was known for her physical prowess and emotional strength. Unscathed by mortal wounds, yet she wore the scars of each battle. She was a warrior. That was all she knew.

She pulled her dagger from her waistband and checked the sharpness of its blade. She was determined to complete her mission.

2014

Moments later, Olivia was fixing her hair in front of the mirror. Her phone rang. She locked the bathroom door and answered the phone. "Hold on." She turned on the bath faucet so Lizzie could not hear her on the phone.

"I can't talk now, but we've got to change the plan! Why? Because we're getting into some serious shit! She's different. Something is off with her. I think she's sick, but I don't know. She could be pregnant." She paused. "If she's pregnant, do you know what that means? It will be terrible if anything goes wrong, and it will be my fault. That will be bad for the both of us. Yes, I'm still going to do it, but I need more time." She ended the call and stared at her distorted reflection in the steamy mirror.
She did not recognize herself. She looked familiar. Face and hair. Nose and lips. But so much had changed so quickly. She hoped it would all come together soon.

1914

On the Montvane Estate, under the full moon, fate crept through time's window, veiled in secrecy. In Olivia's room, the crushing heat of the day gave way to the cool evening breeze that blew through the windows and corridors of the mansion.

As everyone prepared, Olivia shivered with sickness. George Junior sent Jacob to fill her tub with hot water and to fetch Lizzie to tend to her while the rest of the family attended the County Ball.

When Lizzie arrived, Olivia removed the cloth from her forehead and sat upright in the bed.

"George Junior sent word you were sick?"

"I'm fine. I am sick of the County Ball. The heavy dresses and the high hair. Everyone puts on such airs. I despise it"

"What if George Junior finds out?" Lizzie knew how White people's lies could turn Black lives into collateral damage.

"He doesn't scare me. I do have my own mind, Lizzie. He's not my father. Besides, I'm almost 18."

"Why you got to lie then?" Lizzie asked.

Olivia disappeared into the bathing room.

Lizzie followed her. Her eyes were drawn to the new tub perched on four lion's paws.

"You like it. It's an early birthday gift. Mother had it made especially for me and shipped in from Italy."

Lizzie was mesmerized by the sculptured marble tub. "It's so pretty! Don't look like no tub I ever washed in. So big, you can sit down and stretch out your legs to touch your toes."
She gingerly touched the edge of the tub.

"The water is just right. Feel it." Olivia added.

Slowly, Lizzie stuck her fingertip in the water.

"Elizabeth Lucille, I have a splendid idea. You can take my bath!"

Lizzie backed out of the room. "Oh no, I'd better get home."

Olivia pulled her back into the room. "Come on, Lizzie. I shan't tell, and neither shall you. It'll be our secret. You're my only friend. When else will you ever get the chance to bathe like White folks?"

They laughed.

"Got a bit of father's whiskey. Here, taste it." Olivia passed her the snifter while Lizzie relaxed in the warm water.

Olivia and Lizzie sang their secret song, "Like a flower that busies the bee. Like the air all around, we can't see. Bonded by blood, eternally. Sisters forever, you and me."

They were startled by a voice on the other side of the door. "Olivia?!"

Olivia's voice was muted past the point of fear. She could not respond.

"Olivia, are you okay in there?" George Junior asked. He could hear movement in the room, "Is someone in there with you?"

The door flew open. Half-naked, Lizzie ran past George Junior, down the stairs, and out the back door.

He chased her into the woods and tackled her before she reached the line of trees that marked her family's property. He struggled to free himself from his pants. "That's why you ain't gave me none? You a bulldagger? Well, you're going to give me some tonight."

Lizzie kicked and screamed.

While in the barn tending to the horses, Frank heard Lizzie's screams and ran to her rescue.

"What in the devil are you doing? Let go of her!"

"This Black wench. I caught her naked in Olivia's tub."

"Get off of her, George!" Frank wrestled his older brother off the young woman.

She ran as fast as she could through the woods to her house. Frank followed, and Lizzie's father appeared on the porch with his shotgun just as he approached.

"Sir, I wanted to make sure Lizzie's alright?"

The man's crooked back straightened. "I want you and your family to leave my Lizzie alone. You stay away from her, you hear me!"

Frank stormed through the dark woods and up the hill back to the Montvane Estate.

Frank retreated to his bedroom to think. His options were few. His brother's temper and taste for nastiness were rivaled only by his father, George Senior, and his proclivities for the same.

Frank said a prayer hoping for a plan.

Down the hill, Lizzie sat in her room, crying. She stared at Frank's picture in the moonlight and cried herself to sleep.

Two nights later, after exchanging notes left hidden in the big tree in the field, Frank and Lizzie met by the main road and disappeared into the night.

2014

It was a bright, early morning, and the Presidential Building buzzed with activity, the hallway packed with reporters and news crews.

Detective Parker arrived and demanded an explanation, "What the hell is going on in here?"

"Looks like church on Easter Sunday," Detective Bryant chimed in.

"Let's go, people! This is a crime scene."

Detective Parker pulled a uniformed officer to the side, "Get these people in the elevators and out of here. Only necessary police personnel are allowed on this floor."

Parker moved toward a stubborn congregation at the end of the hall. Bryant followed.

"I want this building locked down, now!" Detective Parker exclaimed.

Jones was at the end of the hallway, flanked by news cameras.

A news reporter asked, "Is it true that the suspect is a rogue Bureau agent?"

Parker and Bryant approached the assembly. "Turn those damn cameras off. Broadcast anything, and I will have all of your asses arrested! Get the hell out of here, right now!" Parker demanded.

The group scattered.

Parker approached Jones, "What's your fucking problem?"

"This is the biggest story in the country. It's all over the news. A rogue Bureau agent, dead County officials. C'mon Parker, we've got to give the people something! This is our 15 minutes of fame, brother!"

"I ain't your brother!" Parker barked back.

"You know what they're going to do. They're going to come in and take over. You gonna let them steal your glory again?"

Parker moved in on Jones.

Bryant stepped between them.

"Do you hear this? And they say I'm the one who needs therapy." exclaimed Parker.

"Oh, that's right, I forgot. They took your balls a long time ago." replied Jones.

Detective Bryant was now fully pissed off, "You're out of line, Jones!"

Parker took another step toward Jones, then stopped. "You're off this case. Get the hell out of here."

"Screw you! You're nothing but a washed up, burnt-out, drunk ass– "

Bryant yoked him by the collar and slammed him into the wall next to the elevators. "One more word, and it'll be a crime scene in a crime scene."

"Calm down, church boy, let him go. He's not worth a wrinkle in your suit."

Bryant slowly relaxed his grip and let Jones loose, shoving him into the open elevator.

Moments later, the elevator doors opened to deliver another set of sleuths. Agent Miles Connor and his wife, Agent Brown, exited the elevator.

"Miles Connor," Detective Parker addressed the tall, blond man.

"Stanley Parker," responded Agent Connor, "the dead has been resurrected." he added.

"And in the middle of absolute bedlam." added Detective Parker.

The teams exchanged greetings and handshakes.

"This is my old partner. We used to fight the forces of evil together," Agent Connor announced to the team.

"Save the charm for later, Miles. We've got work to do." stated Parker.

2014

A regular volunteer, Bryant would visit the church soup kitchen twice a week around lunchtime. On this day, however, he entered the church and darted toward a room in the church's basement. He opened the door and was pushed face-first against the wall with his hands behind his back.

"So, is that your idea of romance?" asked Lizzie.

"What's wrong?" he asked.

"A heads up would have been nice. We're supposed to be partners." She tightened her grip on him.

"What are you talking about?"

"They came for me last night."

"What? I didn't know. What happened? They didn't hurt you, did they?"

She released her grip on him. "I'm still standing. But my senses are down, and I don't know what they'll try next."

"I don't like this, Lizzie. If anything happens to you —"

"If we don't go through with the plan, we'll never be free." Lizzie reminded him.

"Maybe it's too much for you right now?"

"Right now? Life's always been dangerous for me," she added.

He grabbed her. "Listen to me. I can't risk anything happening to you. You haven't been yourself lately. Clearly, something is going on with you," he complained, "but you won't let me take you to a doctor or anything."

"No, we have to do this first."

"But Lizzie, it's more than just our lives at stake now. I'm just saying maybe we should abort?"

She pulled away. "You're just saying what? You think we should abort the mission or–"

"The mission, of course." He grabbed her and held her close.

"I'll do it alone if I have to," she told him.

"Why don't you trust me?" he asked her.

"What do you mean?"

"You never told me about your sister." Bryant said.

"I was going to tell you."

"At this point, I think I should know what's going on with you, right?"

She nodded. "I'm sorry. I'm used to being –"

"Private and closed off. I know, but you gotta trust me, Elizabeth."

"Okay. You're sure that's all you want to say?"

He kissed her. "Absolutely." He kissed her again.

"You're sure?"

"Oh yes, there is one more thing. I loved you the first time I saw you, and I want to spend the rest of this life and all my lives with you."

She relaxed in his affection. They kissed. Then, Bryant headed to his car while Lizzie slipped out of the church's back door.

2014

Parker pulled up to the curb in front of the church moments later. "Been looking for you, church boy."

"Well, you found me," answered Detective Bryant.

"Needed a little noonday prayer, huh?"

"Yes. You should've come in and prayed, too."

"No. That's your thing."

"God is for all."

"Tell that to Judge Stafford."

"What are you talking about?" Bryant asked.

"A third victim," replied Parker. "The judge was found this morning at the Presidential. We need to get back there right now."

"I'll meet you there."

"No way. You're like a ghost lately. I need to keep my eyes on you. Get in."

Media trucks and journalists were setting up live remotes outside the police barricade as Parker and Bryant approached the Presidential Building.

2014

Mr. Levine made himself comfortable on Sassie's sofa. When she was alive, she would invite him into the kitchen for chicken and dumplings or three sisters soup, and he would spread their stock projections across the table and all the kitchen counters. She would light sage, sing, dance, and chant before looking at or touching the papers. He remembered the smell of the sage, and how the house would seem to quake when she danced.

He opened his briefcase and handed Lizzie, Olivia, and Ben copies of the will. He asked, "How have the three of you been making out?"

Lizzie answered, "Day by day."

Mr. Levine continued, "Olivia, it's nice to see you back home. The wife sent her love and wants you all over for dinner soon. Sassie was a great business partner and one of our dearest friends. We miss her so."

"We miss her, too," Ben added.

"I have another appointment, so let's get right to it. Sassie had a talent for the stock markets and made many excellent investments and, of course, along with the inheritance from her family, she left a sizable estate. The primary residence, the stables, the farm, and the 200 acres of land upon which it sat were left to the three of you. Lizzie is the executor per Sassie's instructions. The remaining 107,000 acres, including the docks, the upper basin marina, and the Presidential Building, belong to the three of you."

They signed the papers, and the lawyer carried on with informing the family, "The residual income from the land tenants sits in a collective trust for the three of you to draw from as you need. The interest on the accounts pays the taxes and provides more than enough for any future investments you all may decide to make. Also, Sassie left, to be equally divided among the three of you, liquid assets of over 727 million dollars." Mr. Levine collected the signed papers and rose to leave, "They tried to deny her, and she outsmarted them at their own game. Everything she touched turned to gold. My dear Yedidah... I'm blessed to have known her."

They sat in silence for a moment after the attorney left. Ben broke the silence. "So, all those papers we signed mean we're rich?"

2014

In Lizzie's bedroom, the late-night news channel looped footage and sound bites detailing the history of Suffolk County. Special features highlighted the world leaders and billionaire business magnates rumored to be residents of the Presidential Building. Olivia sipped her cocktail and looked through Aunt Sassie's old papers while Lizzie sipped hot tea. Olivia finished her drink, poured another, and took a sip. "I miss Aunt Sassie. It seemed like she protected us from all the evil in this County." She took another sip and fumbled through the papers in the box. "Some of these pictures and receipts are over a hundred years old. You never told me about these."

"Nothing to tell. You heard the stories just like I did. Remember how we'd stay up all night long begging Aunt Sassie to tell us more about the old days," Lizzie answered.

"It was funny how she always knew she would live to be a hundred. Where's that letter she left for me?"

"It should be in that trunk," answered Lizzie.

"I don't see it. It's not here." Olivia was drunk and she had grown increasingly agitated with Lizzie as she searched for the letter.

Right before she passed, Aunt Sassie called Lizzie to her bedside to describe precisely what would happen after she died. With her voice fading in and out like the beat of an ancient dunun drum, she instructed Lizzie to create an identical copy of the letter and place it in the trunk. Then, put the original away in a secret place. She told Lizzie how George, vexed by a generational curse, would bring a book to Lizzie on the day of her funeral. Sassie directed her to prepare a book identical to the book Sassie had seen ninety years ago. Sassie remembered every word in that evil book. She remembered all the names, places, and days of terror recorded on its pages. She told Lizzie to place the original copy of the book in the secret place when George brought it to her.

Lizzie followed the plan, preparing the duplicate book before receiving the original.

And just as Aunt Sassie predicted, George begged her to take the book and relieve the torment that had dogged him throughout his life. He thought the book was cursed. Lizzie knew better. The curse was on the people, not the book. Aunt Sassie had taught Lizzie, Olivia, and Ben that curses could be broken. She trained them to feel the Earth's vibrations. To pray and use the wind, the sun, and the glow of the Moon to break curses.

Lizzie placed the copy of the letter in the trunk next to the duplicate of the book George had given her at Aunt Sassie's funeral.

The plan was working, and the bait had been taken. If Aunt Sassie's prophecy was correct, both the duplicate letter and book would turn up soon to reveal the secrets of the County curse.

"Maybe someone broke in and stole it. You think we should call the police?"

"Nope," Lizzie replied nonchalantly.

"I think we should call those detectives."

"No. We're not calling anyone."

Olivia took a sip from her glass. "Damn it, Lizzie! You lost it! You lost my letter!"

"I didn't lose it."

Olivia was devastated. "Well, where the hell is it? Why do you always have to call the shots? You always have to control things. And now, you lost my letter!"

"I think you've had too much to drink."

"Enough to speak my mind."

"Let me make sure I'm getting this right. You didn't come back to speak your mind when Ben and I needed your help, when she was dying. You didn't come back and speak your mind at the funeral. But now, you want to speak your mind? Look, I forgive you. But sounds like to me that you need to forgive yourself. But be sure about one thing when you speak your mind. You left us, Olivia! And don't you ever forget that!"

"I had to find out if he loved me."

"She told you exactly what would happen if you left! She saw it. She warned you."

Olivia began to cry. "I know, but I hoped things would be different. Then, I was ashamed to come back. Before I left, I cursed at her, and I told her I hated her for keeping me from him. When all she did was love me. All she wanted to do was protect me. She begged me not to go. I didn't believe that he would hurt me again." She broke down. "I'm so sorry for treating her that way... and Ben... and you."

Lizzie tried to console her.

"I didn't get the chance to tell her how much I loved her – to thank her for loving me."

"She knew. She understood. Ben and I cried for years after you left. Aunt Sassie would tell us, it's the most natural thing in the world to want to be with your blood, your family, your kinfolk."

"Even with my dad, I had no one to love me. You and Ben had her."

"You had her, too."

"Not like you."

"She loved us all the same, Olivia."

"And that's what's important, huh?" She wiped her eyes and took another drink.

"You were always so different, so special. She couldn't teach me what she taught you. You had the gift."

"Look, Olivia, you're special too. You know what you mean to us. I'm really sorry about the letter. Trust me, I'll make sure that you have it soon."

Lizzie reached for her tea. "But can we talk about it later? I feel sick. I need to get some rest."

"There you go again, always controlling things, but I love you."

"I love you, too," Lizzie proclaimed before she dozed off.

Moments later, Olivia went into the bathroom to make a phone call. "She's asleep. No, Jamie, she doesn't know yet. I can't keep this up too much longer." She heard a noise outside the bathroom door.

Lizzie knocked impatiently at the door. "Hey, open the door. I've got to use the bathroom."

"It's her, I've gotta go."

"What are you doing in there? I've got to go bad," Lizzie added.

Olivia, disconnected the call, and opened the bathroom door.

2014

As night fell over the Presidential Building, agents and detectives processed the crime scene, knocking on doors and questioning the residents and the building's staff. A Bureau agent walked over to Bryant and whispered something in his ear.

He signaled Parker, and they rushed down the hall.

Detective Parker asked, "What's going on?"

"Two more."

"Where?" asked Parker.

"Second floor."

2014

As the detectives took a break a slow, soft melody played for the patrons in the Presidential Lounge.

Agent Connor announced, "A toast to partners!"

Detective Parker chimed in, "You and Carolyn, 16 years, right?"

"Sixteenth anniversary in May. How's your partner?"

"Frank, he's better than most. Impeccably trained. He is a real gentleman. He's like a son to me. I pray he gets a good partner after I'm gone."

"We could use you up at the Bureau."

"I'm leaving after this case."

"Back to Philadelphia?"

"Nope."

"Where to?"

"Not sure," Parker replied as he sipped his drink. "One thing is for sure: I don't have anything to leave behind but bad memories."

"I think about what happened to you a lot. It was rough."

"Life's been rough since the day I was born," replied the detective.

Connor added, "I wish I could've done more to help." He took a swig from his glass.

Parker recalled, "You could have. But you didn't. And once the Bureau sent down the order, no one could've stopped them but God, and that didn't happen."

"I followed orders, Stan. I messed up."

"It was real fucked up. You didn't have my back, and the Bureau didn't stand behind me. I lost my whole family, and nobody gave a damn!" He took another sip of his drink. "I try not to think about it. But guess what? I think about it a lot."

"I owe you an apology."

"Miles, you don't owe me shit." Parker shot back, lighting a cigarette.

"I could reopen the case. Find out what happened."

Parker sighed, "You know what Miles? It seems cosmically improbable that I could help solve so many crimes, bring justice to so many, but I don't have the justice and peace I need. I've learned to leave it alone. Living in the past nearly killed me, so I stay as far away from it as possible."

In silence, the two men collect their thoughts and finish their drinks.

2014

George was frantically trying to explain to the secretary why he had been calling for several days. He had seen the police lock down parts of the building. His muscles were tense. He could not stop sweating, and his stomach churned with trauma. He thought that if he left this apartment, he would not be safe.

"I am calling to cancel my appointment."

Dr. McKay had been George's psychiatrist for the last year. After his most recent breakdown, Dr. McKay recommended that George take the apartment and the job at the Presidential Stables as a caretaker for the horses.

"I can't cancel. This is unbelievable! He's my doctor, not my father, got-damn it! And if I don't want to see him, he can't make me!"

There was a sound outside the door.

The doctor entered. "Close your eyes. Sleep, my son." George fell into a deep trance. After a while, the door slammed behind the man's shadow.

George jumped up and ran to the door. He looked out. The hallway was empty. Dr. McKay was gone. He closed the door. His head ached, and his heart was pounding in his chest. He was unsure if it was the doctor or if his mind was playing tricks on him. That was why the doctor gave him the pills. The haunting visions and memories constantly flashed behind his eyes, lurking under every thought he tried so hard to make pleasant.

Stumbling to the counter, he gulped down two pills and a mouthful of water. He lay across the couch, reached for the remote, and turned on the television.

Breaking news. Something terrible happened in the building again. He was sick of it all. He turned off the television.

"Nothing makes any sense. Not the news. Not my life. Not even this therapy," he pronounced out loud to himself. He needed to talk to someone he could trust. He picked up the phone and dialed Lizzie's number but could not speak when she answered.

He rocked back and forth, trying to counter the powerful effects of the sedatives and the regression therapy that had taken his mind back a hundred years in time. If only he could start over again, he would do things differently. He felt like a traveler lost on a long journey, wishing the trip would end and return him to the point of departure.

2014

Detective Parker and Agent Connor worked with the Bureau's Technology Team all night to set up the task force command center.

A small group of civilians approached. Agent Connor asked, "Can I help you?"

A barrel-chested, older Black man emerged from the center of the small mob. "I am Jacob Giles, Esquire, and the Vice Count of Suffolk County."

Agent Connor responded, "I am Agent Connor. This is a secure command center, and you're in an authorized-only zone. You and your group can wait in the lobby, and I'll have a press release brought out."

The man replied, "I don't think you understand. The Presidential Building is an entity in itself. Dr. McKay, the Count, and I pride ourselves on the history and sovereignty of this County. Agent Connor, you're familiar with our history, so you know what that means." The Vice Count grinned.

"Why don't you tell me what it means." Agent Connor returned the man's grin.

"It means that, unless you have the Count's approval, you and your associates will have to leave this building."

"Look, I don't know who you think you are, but if you think you or some Count can shut down my investigation, you are gravely mistaken."

Parker jumped into the exchange, "Being gravely mistaken will definitely cost your ass. I think you better stay on this guy's good side. You don't want to make him mad."

The Vice Count adjusted his bow tie and cleared his throat.

Agent Connor warned, "You need to leave, do you understand? Because, if not, in 30 seconds I'm going to dial a code into my phone, and when I speak your name, at that very moment, your life will dissolve into thin air. You will no longer exist. Your bank accounts will be closed. Your own mother will claim to have never heard your name. Your entire life will be wiped from the record."

Parker lit a cigarette and watched the Vice Count's face go blank. "The shit 'bout to hit the fan now. Trust me, the Bureau don't play. You'd better get out of here or you can kiss your ass goodbye!"

Connor reached for his phone. The Vice Count turned and led the group out. The doors were locked, and the briefing began. The room lit up with multiple images and charts.

"Good morning, team. Detective Parker is going to bring us all up to speed."

Detective Parker began explaining the points of the case to the Bureau team. "First victim, the County Chaplain Mauritzio Caldena was found dead two days ago. Decapitated in his fifth-floor condo. Second victim, Attorney General Max Frattini, found yesterday morning on the fourth floor. The third victim, the Honorable Judge Vann Stafford of the Supreme County Court, was found yesterday on the third floor. Senator Guerloff Stollemeyer and the County Comptroller, Douglass Jefferson, were also found yesterday on the second floor. There's an order and a pattern to this. The killer has been working from a list. And we're late! This thing is almost done. There are six floors in this building. What in the hell does that tell you? Maybe, we can help the last person on the list keep his head attached to his neck if we move our asses!" Parker glared at everyone in the room for a moment, then he continued, "All five victims appear to have been decapitated with the same type of blade. We're waiting on the toxicology and DNA reports for each victim and scene, and they should be in by noon. Now, I'll let Agent Devell present his findings."

Agent Devell stood, and new charts and images appeared. "There have been several links between the victims, including gender and income. The next link I've listed is relevant to association and location. All the victims were executive members of the County Advisory Board, and they all received offices and private condos in the Presidential as a part of their County honorarium benefits. Consequently, each victim was found dead in said apartment. My team is cross-checking memberships in other clubs and organizations, digital files, phone records, and interviewing family, friends, staff, and business associates. Anyone with ties to the County Board and this building is being run through the system as we speak."

Connor directed the next team member, Agent Garney, to present the report on his team's findings. "My team has been processing several items found at each scene. First, a woman's hair barrette. This piece was custom-made and purchased in the early 1900s. It was expensive then. In today's antique market, it's valued at over 13 million dollars. The hair found in the clasp appears to be of African descent. That hair is being tested for a DNA profile. At the second scene, there was a picture of a Black family. Taken in the early 1900s. At the third scene, a set of pass papers, documents certified by the County Board that identified free Black people. That's all I have for now."

Agent Connor looked toward his wife, "Agent Brown, the floor is yours."

Carolyn Brown stood to attention. Years of military service were evident in her posture and her tone. She had always been outspoken, too outspoken for the Bureau, some thought. It did not take her long to make them aware of her value, and she wore it better than any suit in her closet.

After years of special projects detecting and recording the plantation crimes of the past, she had become an expert in the field of historic forensics. Patrolling the old boys' network that ran the underbelly of Suffolk County, she had helped solve several cases. There were families who would have been pleased to keep and pass down their evil heirlooms and secrets sealed in jars and glass cases; whispered about and kept in attics and back offices; brought out to show at family reunions and parties. These were savage trinkets and hellish treasures, protected by the descendants of demons. Body parts and organs were visual aids with names. Little Millicent's left ear and Ole Joe's penis. All were evidence of the legendary stories of enslaved people's torment.

Agent Brown knew all too well the level of depravity that they were facing. "There are forces among us that are working to stop the progress of equality in this County. It's our job to keep the world moving forward. This as why we are here. We will not allow the hands of time to be turned back. We will not tolerate the infection that threatens this County. This evil must be plucked up from the root."

Connor joined his wife at the front of the room. "Agent Garney's team will continue processing the interior of the building. Agent Devell's team will resume questioning the staff and tenants. Rodgers has a sweep of the grounds covered. Agents Gwen and Bethea will deal with the media. Other teams proceed as usual."

2014

It was morning, and Lizzie sat on the porch sipping hot tea. She noticed a Bureau vehicle driving past. Olivia sauntered onto the porch.

Lizzie handed her a cup of tea. "You were talking in your sleep last night."

"I had a nightmare."

"About what?"

"George."

"My George?"

"Yes. He was running through the basement naked. Screaming at the top of his lungs. There was a man in a black robe chasing him."

"What happened?"

"They ran through the wall."

"What?"

"Like ghosts. Ran through the wall and out back to the woods by the big tree."

"If Aunt Sassie was alive, she could tell you what it means."

Olivia turned to Lizzie. "You can tell me what it means."

Lizzie did not respond. She sat silently sipping her tea.

2014

A few days later, in a television studio miles from the Presidential Building, the producer counted down, "In five... four... three... two..."

The host faced the camera with a dazzling smile.

"Today, our guest is psychiatrist and author Dr. George McKay. Dr. McKay, it's a pleasure to have you here."

"Pleasure to be here."

"First of all, in keeping with the County's 100th anniversary celebration, my producer tells me that you are celebrating your 100th birthday today. That is quite a milestone."

The camera zoomed in for a closeup.

"It is hard to believe. You don't look a day over 50! You must come back and share your secret with our viewers!"

"Many things in this life are hard to believe," the doctor responded.

"Let's talk about your new book D&A: Descendants and Ancestors."

"Many years of research went into this book."

"How did you, a psychiatrist, become interested in genetics?"

The doctor shifted in his chair. "Let me explain it this way: people are like statues cast in a mold. Even though there are many different people in the world. My research proves that there are only six molds or genealogical categories into which each person's personality or behavior fits."

The host queried further, "So your study proposes that there are only six different personality types in the world? Why not five? Why not seven?"

"My epistemology is based on the cycle of six."

"I'm sure a doctor of your esteem would like to explain your system to our viewers?"

"I don't care to discuss that since it is far too complex for the average person to ever understand."

"Could you give a historical accounting for your theory? It may help our viewers understand."

"My accounting was calculated to contain the entire span of human life on this planet, as we know it, with the five senses that most people use."

"What exactly does that mean?"

"It means that it applies to all human existence. Regardless of the age, era, or time as we know it."

"Wow, Okay. That's a sweeping theory, doctor."

"Every human has DNA or a genetic code. This code, if read properly, can tell many things about a person. Physical identifiers, hair color, height, things like that, and that includes psychological predispositions."

"And you are currently working on a new database? Could you tell our viewers about that?"

"Over the next 50 years, the profiles of more than 79% of the population will have been collected by way of medical tests, records, employment, and incarceration. There's also genetic information that can be gleaned from artifacts that have been archived for historical, medical, and research purposes throughout history. My database will analyze, merge, and utilize all these information units to provide psychologistic reports instantaneously."

"Who will have access to your database?"

"Doctors, law enforcement, researchers, policymakers, and other authorized vendors."

"Your critics say that psychologistics are unethical – a type of genetic profiling. A violation of human civil rights."

"My database will revolutionize the field of behavior prediction." The doctor straightened his bowtie. "Most people don't understand the evil of the mind."

"Your past life regression lab was shut down by the International Research Review Board, isn't that right?"

"The sessions were phenomenal. The hypnosis brought up memories more vivid than reality and more supernatural than any dream or nightmare."

"Patients and their families filed complaints against you."

"Sacrifice must always be made for progress."

"Many of your colleagues question the ethics of your research methods."

He thought to himself, how dare she bother him with the pathetic jealousies of inferior minds. "What they choose to ignore is the fact that the information is there. It has already been collected. Now, it must be interpreted and used."

The theme music signaled the end of the show.

"That's all for our show today. Join us for next week's show. Dr. George McKay will join us again for a roundtable discussion on DNA privacy protections. Hopefully, Dr. McKay will share more about the essence of his psychologistics theory and database. Thanks for tuning in. We'll see you next week."

The host extended a hand to Dr. McKay.

He pulled her close and whispered in her ear. "You moronic bitch, I am a pioneer. I have lived to see lesser men come and go." He ripped the microphone from his lapel and stormed out of the studio.

2014

Dr. McKay bypassed the Bureau's checkpoint and barricades at the Presidential Building. He drove down the overgrown, little used back road that leads to the old stables. He left the car parked behind the stables. He unlocked a door in the back of the stables that opened to a hallway and a private staircase leading up to his office.

Moments later, inside his office, barely stifling his indignation, he poured himself a drink. He summoned the Vice Count to his office.

Jacob entered and handed Dr. McKay a box of cigars. "A gift for your birthday."

The doctor set the box on his desk and stood to look out of the window. "Jacob, this has always been my territory. I don't like the Bureau snooping around up here. It upsets the balance of things."

"They don't care about County sovereignty anymore, boss man. Times have changed."

"That's what they say, but I– I truly know how times have changed. I know about changing times!" The doctor laughed. "Have a drink with me. Relax, Jacob. I want to talk to you. I am sure you have a moment for your old comrade."

The office was quiet except for the clock on the desk clicking with each second, counting the time. The doctor poured Jacob a drink. Jacob took a slow, cautious sip.

"Drink. Enjoy. I've been saving this bottle for a very, very long time."

Jacob sipped again.

"Remember my first week in this office. Two days without a secretary and Betsy appeared like magic. You remember her, don't you? She was dedicated. She would take work home, so she didn't have to stay late – so she could spend more time with her husband and the two children. Do you remember her, Jacob? My research began to take on a life of its own. The stories were exquisite beyond my wildest imagination." The doctor laughed.

Jacob was still.

"Remember the notes that I gave her to transcribe, Jacob. She came in the next day with that terrible look on her face. I knew I had made a horrible mistake. I assured her that she had misread. That she was overworked. I couldn't let the secret be revealed, not then." The doctor laughed again and took a sip of his ancient drink. I convinced her that she and the children would have fun at the party. After the party, she would get plenty of rest, and those horrible stories that she had misread would fade from her memory. Jacob, do you remember the party?"

Jacob remained perfectly still, but he responded "The party. There was no party."

"Good boy. You've always been such a good boy. Such an obedient servant." He patted Jacob's head.

"I could have just hypnotized her to forget what she had read. But it was entertaining – watching her face when I asked her about the notes. You could tell she didn't want to repeat it. She wanted to say, 'Go to hell, you murderer,' but she couldn't. Hypnosis, the power to control another person's behavior. Now, that is an ancient technology that many people don't understand, much less appreciate. I know you enjoyed it, too, Jacob. But it was no party for her or the little boy – just lots to clean up afterward. I don't know how you do it. There's no way I could've cleaned up all that blood by myself. You have always been such a good helper. You know something, I wanted the little girl, too. I knew it was a mistake to leave her alive. It would have been better if I had got all three and shut down the bloodline."

Jacob was still.

The doctor slammed his hand on the desk. "I can't take it, Jacob! They're talking against me. They don't believe what I know. Damn it, they don't understand what I have seen, and they don't know what I can do."

He stared at Jacob for a moment before he sat. He opened the box of cigars, took one and lit it before continuing, "And now that I have the book back in my possession no one can stop me, and the letter is icing on the cake. It's been a long time coming. You know what I'm most afraid of? Being a dinosaur, a relic. We have lived so many lives. I miss how things used to be, don't you, Jacob?"

Jacob remained still.

The doctor laughed at how easily he executed his hypnotic craft. He snapped his fingers.

Jacob took another sip from his glass. "This is superb. What year is it?"

"1914, from my personal collection to celebrate the County Centennial."

"Very smooth, sneaks up on you. Aren't you going to open your gift? Wait, when did you open the–"

"Do you mind? I have work to do."

"Did I miss something? I thought you wanted to talk," Jacob asked.

"My social mood has passed."

Jacob stood, "Alright, whatever you say, boss man."

1896

The door swung open, and Isabelle Montvane entered the County Church for the evening service. She strolled up the aisle to the front row of the church. The service resumed and finished with the members singing the last hymn.

The church emptied.

Reverend Elijah Walker, a tall, muscular young man, clutched his Bible and stepped down from the pulpit.

"Bless you for coming, Sister Montvane."

"I'm sorry I missed the start of your sermon. I was late getting dressed."

Beautifully dark and stunning, Rose Long Hope appeared out of the shadows of the pulpit. Her long, black braids wrapped gracefully around her head like a halo. "How are you, Sister Montvane?"

"Fine."

"And your husband?"

"Fine."

"That's a lovely dress."

"Designed and shipped in from Spain. The same as my gown for the Ball tonight."

"I'm sure you'll be the prettiest lady there."

Isabelle was powerful but not pretty. She was well-known but not liked. Everything that Isabelle was not, Rose was. Isabelle knew it, and she hated Rose for it.

"I love the way you read the word, Reverend."

"God's word is a good thing to love. We all read at Bible study. You should come sometimes."

"I prefer to study in secret," she remarked. She was three years old when her family fled to America 30 years ago. Born Isabella Camilla Alejandra. Promised to him by her father, she married Master George Montvane of Suffolk when she was 15. She replaced the 'a's with 'e's and proudly wore her new name, Isabelle Camille Montvane, like the blond wigs and pale cosmetics she required.

"My husband will be announcing your appointment at the Ball tonight. The Board wants to celebrate with you." She put her hand on his arm. "I left my purse up the hill. I will give you my offering tonight."

"Sister Montvane, you have given so much, the church is truly thankful."

"Time will tell, Reverend. I'll be expecting you tonight."

She left, and Elijah closed the door behind her. Elijah and Rose moved among the benches, cleaning and preparing the church for tomorrow's Bible study. "Rose, you need to rest. I'll finish up out here," he said, walking over to her as she let out a long yawn.

"If you are tired, our little one must be tired, too." He rubbed her stomach and kissed her gently, savoring the sweetness of her lips.

"Do you have to go?" Rose asked.

"I must go. I have been chosen."

1896

Preparing for the County Ball conjured up memories of how he had grown up in the hills of Kentucky. Desperate for a better life, he left the small town of his birth. Traveling penniless was a course in survival. Before he came to the County, his good looks and charisma had kept hunger away more than a few times. Now, his skin urged benefits from the wealthy, but in their eyes, his poverty was still cause for distance. With recommendation and desperation, Elijah accepted the offer to pastor the church in Suffolk.

As he walked up the hill to the Ball, he wondered how her husband dealt with her. He had heard stories. In a place like this, with people like them, there were always stories.

"Having fun?"

"Yes, Sister Montvane."

As hated as she was, she was beguiling. Her sexuality barely restrained beneath her clothing.

"Please, call me Isabelle." She summoned drinks for them.

"The music is nice."

"Can a preacher dance?" she asked

"The Bible said David danced. I can't. Rose says I dance like a fish out of water." They laughed.

"All you need is someone to show you how to do it. Then, you do it over and over again."

"Some things can only be helped with prayer."

Again, they laughed. She not as much.

"Elijah, I want to show you something." She grabbed his hand, "Come this way."

The music grew faint as she pulled him deeper into the belly of the building. He followed her to the end of a long, dark hallway. She opened the door to a room. A large mahogany desk sat in the center. The matching paneled walls shined to mirrored perfection.

"This must be your husband's study?"

"It is," she answered gently.

"What does he do?" he asked as he admired the room.

"Whatever he wants to do. His family's money came from three plantations. One in the County and two outside of Williamsburg. Got sharecroppers farming most of the plantation land now. But George threw himself into buying the best livestock, running moonshine, munitions, motors, tobacco and, of course, he's still a cotton man."

"Business must be good."

She smiled, "This is for you," reaching into her bosom, she handed him an envelope and backed him into the desk.

The room became smaller.

"We Montvanes don't mind sharing. We're very generous." She purred and rubbed her body against his.

"Sister Montvane, please stop."

"It'll be our secret."

"Please stop. It's a sin. I couldn't. I'm a man of God."

"No one will know but us."

He tried to resist, but it was too late. His manhood was in her hands. His willpower was no match for her lust. She finished quickly.

She smiled, dismounted him, and fixed her dress.

The music from the Ball followed him all the way back down the hill to the little church. He hoped Rose was not awake. He quietly entered the small room at the back of the church. He pulled off his clothes to lie down on the cot beside Rose. He shut his eyes tightly to pray.

Elijah silently asked God, "How could this have happened to me again?" The night after the Arkansas revival arose in his mind. It had happened while sharing a tent with a preacher from Tennessee. It was as if he was reliving the most horrible night of his life on the road. But, this time, the violator was a woman.

1896

Months later, Rose gave birth to their baby in the back of the church where she and Elijah slept. She named their baby girl Heather. One morning, Rose awoke to nurse Heather. She reached for her, but the baby was gone.

"Elijah! Elijah, where's Heather?" She searched desperately in every corner of the church for the tiny newborn. The woman started frantically screaming, "Where's my baby?! Why are you just standing there? We must find her! Run up the hill and ask Sister Montvane for help. Please, Elijah, go now!"

"No, Rose, we shouldn't bother them. It won't help. Besides, Sister Montvane left this morning on a train to New York. She won't be back for six months."

"My Heather! My precious Heather! You must find our Maanipokaa!" She begged Elijah to get the sheriff.

The sheriff came and declared, "Nothing I can do about it. Maybe Indians ran off with the baby." The sheriff laughed.

Rose cried.

1897

With the passing of another year, the County Board celebrated at the Montvanes' Ball. Isabelle hurried over to Elijah with an extra drink in hand. "I wasn't sure you'd come. Here, have a drink with me."

"I can't keep doing this."

"Please, Elijah."

"If your husband caught us, he would have me lynched."

"Nonsense, you're not a nigger."

"To your husband, I may as well be."

"Fine. Come with me. Let me get my purse, and you can be on your way, Reverend Walker! It will only take a moment."

She led him down the long, dark hallway to her husband's study, away from the party goers and the servants. She wanted him and attacked him with all her strength. He slapped her. The violence excited her. She proclaimed, "I love you!"

The room spun around him. "But it's wrong. You're a married woman, and I'm a married man!"

She laughed in his face, "You're a *White* man! All Rose could ever be is your savage whore!"

"In God's eyes, she is my wife."

She strolled over to the bar and poured herself a shot of whiskey. "I'm with child."

"What about your husband?" he asked.

"Oh, you haven't heard?" She laughed, "This is not my husband's child. The town folks say he got into an awful scuffle with a slave girl when he was a boy. That coon cut the whole thing off." She turned to him, "I would like to make a confession, Reverend. George can't make babies. He ain't got no nature. We act like he does, or at least, I have to act like he does, and in exchange for my acting, he gives me whatever I want."

She tried to embrace him.

"What about George Junior?"

"A junior only in name. But he has certainly taken on the ways of George Senior." She tried to touch him again. "Now that I'm having your baby, everything will be perfect. Don't you see?"

"You must stop this!" He pulled away from her, sobbing. "God, what have I done? Who have I become? Don't you think I'm tortured enough with your wicked deals? Your bribery?" he cried.

"I'm wicked? I'll wager that your sweet Rose would love to know how you traded your baby for that Clydesdale."

He grabbed her by the arm and pulled her close to him.

"If we repent, the Lord will be just to forgive us."

"Well, so much for that. I must say you do make a beautiful baby girl, but maybe our baby will be a boy."

Her pleasure was the agony of his destiny. Each year, the affair brought more ransom and more privilege. The benefits matured as the children grew older. Cattle, horses, and land, a motorized Wagoner, gold and silver bars, jewelry – wealth beyond anything Reverend Walker had ever imagined.

1914

It was evening at the Montvane Estate, and the members arrived in long, black robes. The barn was lit with candles. A young Black boy was tied up in the corner.

George Senior announced, "Prepare to take the oath of the Sons of Suffolk."

Each man, as his name was called, stood in the center of the ritual and took his turn repeating the vow.

"Repeat after me," led George Senior.

"I, Mauritizio Caldena, swear to keep the secrets of the Board in confidence..."

"I, Maxwell Frattini, ...vow to advance our ends with souls..."

"I, Vann Stafford, ...vow to sacrifice the blood of sons..."

"I, Guerloff Stollemeyer, ...vow to pledge loyalty to the County..."

"I, Douglass Jefferson, ...vow to sign this record in blood..."

"I, George Montvane Junior, ...vow to keep the secret deeds as they were written..."

George Senior finished the vow, "It is as it shall be." He grabbed a handful of the boy's hair and swung the blade. The boy's body collapsed to the ground. He placed the boy's head in a tin tub. He touched each of the men's foreheads with the thick, warm blood.

The men dispersed to meet and celebrate their secret ceremony at the Ball.

The young George could hardly contain himself. It was such a shame Olivia would not be joining the family that night at the Ball. He loved to see her primped and fresh in her feminine fineries. She was beautiful; distant, though. The thought of her distance added anger to his excitement, making the pressure surging beneath his waist grow stronger. She and Frank were close. He was his father's favorite son, but Frank was Olivia's favorite brother. Now, Olivia and Frank would both have to submit to him.

"Everyone must do as I say now, right father? Olivia and Frank, too?"

"Yes, now that you know the secret, you can control anyone you want."

"I'm a real Suffolk County man."

"Yes. A fine Southern gentleman. So, now the book goes to you."

"I understand." George Junior replied.

"And the blade." George Senior reminded him.

"I'm not afraid." added George Junior.

"I'll get Jacob to clean up this mess in the morning." remarked George Senior.

He took out a flask and shared it with Junior. "There is one more thing we must do."

They buried the boy's head next to the big tree in the field. "Let's get to the Ball. Your mother will be upset if I miss her favorite waltz."

1914

Betsy and Rose sat on the front porch sipping tea. "Sure is bright out here today," Betsy commented.

"Clear enough to see all the way out to the big tree," added Rose.

Reverend Walker stepped onto the porch, buttoning up his clergyman's cape. "Thought I heard you two out here. Betsy, how are you today?"

"Thankful the Lord has given us another day to repent," Betsy replied sternly.

Elijah turned his attention to Rose. "How do I look in my new cloak?"

"Fit to marry," responded Rose.

He stepped off the porch. "The altar calls."

"Will it be late when you return?" Rose asked.

"How many times do I have to tell you the same thing, Rose? God's time is not our time!" He left the two women on the porch and headed to the chapel.

"It is a pretty day," said Rose.

"It's a sad day," replied Betsy.

"Who are we to judge?" Rose asked.

"Evil must be judged," Betsy answered.

"Elijah prays for them to change."

"Too much evil already done." Betsy's mouth sours, and her stomach churned, thinking about the things she knew about the Montvanes.

"God's grace is for all," Rose added.

The wedding processional moved up the hill from the chapel. Rose and Betsy left the porch and walked toward the road with the others to watch the passing pomp. Elijah led the wedding party riding atop his newest Arabian horse, a gift from the Montvanes for performing the marriage. The people pointed and stared. The bride and groom sat like statues in the carriage. The bride turned toward Rose, and her face revealed a horrible secret.

It was Heather.

1914

Days later, Rose gathered the strength to travel up the hill. This was her first time at this door. She knocked, and a young Black girl opened the door and led Rose into the sitting room.

Isabelle stood and asked, "Rose, what are you doing up here?"

Rose looked closely at the tall, handsome young man who was standing at the far side of the room, watching her.

"Franklin, stop staring," barked Isabelle. "Go and get her something cold to drink. It's a long way up that hill."

The young man's face was familiar to Rose, and his manner was the same.

"I've seen you in town. I've always wondered about your people, especially those names. What's your name?"

"Did you hear me, Franklin? Have one of the servants get her something cold to drink. It's hot as the devil today."

"Yes, Mother. Excuse my manners, Ma'am," the young man said before leaving the room.

"He's just like his father. He'll talk to any old thing that'll stand still."

The young man returned with a glass of cold lemonade. Rose took the glass from his familiar-looking hand.

"Long Hope," she said.

"Excuse me, Ma'am?"

"My name is Rose Long Hope," the woman explained.

Heather entered the room. Her eyes frantically scanned the room. "Mother?"

Both women responded, "Yes?"

"Olivia, what are you looking for?" asked Isabelle.

"I can't find my poncho."

"Good. Dreaded thing. I hated it. I hate them all!" Isabelle explained.

"You can have this one." Rose walked over to the beautiful eighteen-year-old. She removed her poncho and wrapped it around the young woman's shoulders. Rose wanted to grab her and hold her; take her back down the hill and tell her the truth. Holding back tears, she stepped away.

"It is so soft and beautiful, and it smells so sweet." Olivia held the fabric close to her face. There was something comforting in its smell. "What is that fragrance? Is it heather?"

"Yes, it is... Heather."

"It smells heavenly, thank you," with gratitude, she embraced Rose, "I shall never take it off."

Rose left the old Clydesdale she had ridden up the hill tied outside the Montvane's door. She cried as she walked back down to the bottom of the hill to return home.

The Reverend sat in his chair, reading his Bible.

She slapped his face hard.

"Rose, please forgive me. I am so sorry!" He begged.

She never said another word to him. Now, she knew the rumors were true. They were real flesh and blood stories. After a few days, fearing she might poison him or cut his throat in his sleep, Reverend Walker took what he could fit into his bag and left the County.

Life began anew for Rose. Her shattered heart was miraculously mended. By the next summer, she was married and expecting a child. Finally, Rose felt happy again. Seven months later, she died while giving birth to her second daughter, Sassie.

1914

Months later, Frank and Lizzie returned to the Montvane Estate to plan their next trip. Abroad, Frank and Lizzie worked hard to secure buyers for crops so the entire County would profit. They were bringing the business of the old plantation into a new era of fair land sharing and exporting.

Lizzie was excited to see Olivia.

"Sister, I have missed you so. How are things with you?"

"You didn't answer any of my letters. I needed you, Lizzie."

"I never got any letters."

"I gave them to George Junior to send off," Olivia poured herself a drink. "But never mind that now."

"What's wrong?" Lizzie asked.

"Nothing's wrong. Look, I'm married." They marveled at the sparkling ring perched on her ring finger.

"I didn't think there was any man your father would ever approve of. I can't wait to meet him. Where is he?"

The door swung open. George Junior stood grinning at Lizzie, "Haven't seen you in a spell. What's wrong? You look like you've seen the devil himself."

Lizzie realized what had happened. To her it felt like time stood still in this little County with its big problems and small minds.

"I've got to go." Lizzie slid past George Junior and ran home.

1914

Frank and Lizzie met in the field the next day under the big tree. Lizzie pulled away from him. Frank, protesting, tried to hold her.

She pulled further away.

"We leave for Europe Friday, and we will never come back to this madness. We're going far away from here. Soon, you will be my wife." He tried again to pull her close. "We will have our own family."

"Not now," Lizzie told him, "I can't."

Frank leaned against the tree, feeling faint. "This has nothing to do with us, Lizzie. My family – you know I'm not like them. There's no telling what Olivia has gone through while we were away. Think of Olivia. Think of me. Please don't do this, Lizzie."

She remained silent.

"Please don't do this, not to my heart, not to our future." He was devastated. "I would never hurt you. I love you too much!"

She replied slowly, "I love you, too."

He begged her again to forgive him for the horror of his family. He was desperate. "What about the baby?"

She did not answer. She silently turned away and headed to her family's home.

He knew better than to follow her there.

1914

The next day, Lizzie was sitting on the porch reading. She saw Olivia coming down the path through the trees. She rushed to meet her away from the porch.

"What are you doing down here?"

"You are the only one I can talk to. I miss you."

"I miss you, too, but–"

"After you and Franklin left, I don't know what happened. It's like I was under a spell. They're evil. I'm not like them. I want to leave, too, Lizzie. Franklin, you, and I... We could all leave and never come back. Franklin has it all figured out. He's got a plan. It's a good plan, Lizzie."

"I can't."

Lizzie left Olivia crying in the grassy clearing under the big tree. She looked across the field at her only friend before closing the door to her family's house.

2014

In the early afternoon there was a knock at the door. Lizzie answered, "Hello. Come in. Nice to finally meet you! Olivia, your friend is here," Lizzie yelled toward the kitchen. "You're Jamie, right?"

"And you're Lizzie?" the woman asked.

"Yes, I am. Have a seat and make yourself at home."

Olivia emerged from the kitchen. She was stunned. "What are you doing here?!"

"Sorry, I was worried about you. You haven't been answering your phone. I had to be sure you were Okay."

"I told you, 'no.' I'm not ready for this! It's not the right time!"

"Relax, Olivia," Lizzie chimed in.

"Something smells really good. What is that?" the woman wondered.

"That's Aunt Sassie's recipe. You should stay and have dinner with us. Don't you want some chicken and dumplings?"

"Lizzie, not now," warned Olivia.

"Will it help if I tell you that I know?"

"You know what?" asked Olivia.

"You've been sneaking around, whispering on the phone, trying to hide that you're gay."

"I didn't want to push you away," replied Olivia.

"You can't push me away. We're family. I love you more than that."

1914

The full moon cast a spell of shadows. George Junior saw Lizzie walking through the field. He grabbed her from behind. She fought hard, but he pulled her into the dark barn. He was instantly on top of her.

She fought to try to get loose. Her mouth was pressed to the ground. Dirt muffled her screams. He slammed his fist into the back of her head, knocking her unconscious. He pulled up the back of her dress and plunged into her.

In the darkness behind him, Olivia raised a shovel and slammed it into the back of his head.

George collapsed.

Lizzie came to.

"Go, Lizzie! Go now!"

Trembling and terrified, Lizzie clutched Olivia's hand. They cried and hugged for a second, then Lizzie ran toward the trees. Olivia dropped the bloody shovel, straightened her dress and stepped over George's body to return to the main house.

2014

Night had fallen over the County, and Olivia and Jamie were clearing the dinner table, when there was a knock at the door.

Lizzie answered it. "George, come in."

"Lizzie, where's the book? I need the book!"

"Calm down, George. Everything will be fine."

"I'm sorry I treated you badly."

"You were sick, George. You couldn't help it."

"I'm ashamed. He keeps taking my mind back to that plantation," George said before he collapsed.

The women gathered him up and placed him on the couch.

"I was made to sacrifice," he said over and over again.

"I think we should call a doctor." Olivia said.

"No doctor! Too many deals in the darkness. You have secrets, too. Is the blood easy for you, Lizzie?" George asked.

She directed Olivia. "He's delirious. Get a cold cloth."

"Where's the book, Lizzie? I need that book! You promised you'd keep it safe!"

"Calm down, George."

"He's coming for us."

"I know." Lizzie replied

"He's evil."

Olivia returned and handed Lizzie a cool, wet cloth.

"Lie still, George. It'll be alright," Lizzie assured him.

"It's like déjà vu. Seems like we've been here before." cried George.

There was a noise in the basement. "I'll check it out," volunteered Jamie.

"I'm going with you," added Olivia. The two women descended the back staircase.

"It has to be finished, Lizzie. We have to see it through. It is the destiny of the County – the book, the vow, and the blade."

Lizzie could hear the doctor coming up the back steps. He entered the room and pointed his gun at her and George. "Come with me."

Detective Bryant watched through the window as the doctor pointed the gun at Lizzie and followed her down the back staircase.

The doctor tied Lizzie's hands behind her back and left her next to Olivia and Jamie. "We all have an appointment with destiny tonight. The oath must be fulfilled. This work has taken lifetimes. We have all returned to see it through."

1914

George Senior entered the barn. He heard a voice pleading, "Help me."

"Who's there?" George Senior asked.

"Over here," replied George Junior. The man could see a figure lying on the barn floor. He moved closer. The back of George's head was bleeding, and his face was twisted.

"What happened to you son?"

"Lizzie," he mumbled.

"That Black heifer. I should've broken her in a long time ago myself. She would have been easier to control. Would've saved you the trouble."

"Fetch Jacob, he'll fix me up."

"First, let me get you up to the main house." George Senior tried to help him to his feet.

In the pale moonlight, George Junior could see the man's frailty. He pulled away from him, "Get Jacob!"

The man went to the barn door and whistled a code, calling Jacob to meet him in the barn.

"Okay. I've called for him. Let me help you, son."

"Don't touch me, old man." George Junior struggled to sit upright.

"Junior, you need to take your time."

"I'll take my time. I know the secrets. I know the truth. One day, this will all be mine. Your time is up."

"Your head's not right. You're hurt bad!"

"You're no man, Master Montvane, with all your nasty secrets. I will tell it all and pray for your soul once everyone in the County knows the deals you make with the Devil."

George Senior grabbed the bloody shovel from the barn floor and swung it hard.

Several minutes later, Frank entered the barn.

"What are you doing out here so late, father?" Coming closer, he caught sight of George Junior, a bloody heap on the barn floor.

Master Montvane lit a cigar and took a swig from his flask as Jacob arrived. Frank knelt next to George Junior to try to help.

"It's too late. He's dead."

"Who did this?"

"The way I see it, it's your fault. If it wasn't for you and that Black bitch you think is so special."

"How am I or Lizzie to blame?"

"Never mind that now. Jacob and I are going to round up the gang."

George Senior took another sip from his flask and passed it to Jacob.

"This doesn't make any sense." said Frank.

"You damn right, it doesn't make sense! I wish you were the one lying here dead instead of Junior."

Frank began to pray next to George's body. "God have mercy on our souls."

With his hand on his pistol, the old man warned, "Shut your mouth and get out of here, or I'll lay you out right next to him."

By the time Frank made it back to the main house, it was too late to stop what would happen.

1914

The horses were excited by the late night commotion. "I told you. I don't know nothing 'bout what you're sayin'," said Lizzie's father.

The snow began to fall.

Guerloff Stollemeyer replied, "Stanley, the man's son is dead."

Douglass Jefferson added, "And you know someone's got to pay."

"It just ain't right when White folk turn up dead. We know your daughter had trouble with him before, but you can't think that you could do what a White man could do," added Vann Stafford.

The snowfall started coming down heavier and quicker.

Lizzie's father responded, "I told you I ain't touched your son. But if your son touched my daughter again. I thank God that he's dead."

"He's not going to 'fess up to it. Let's hang these coons and get it over with," said George Senior.

Crouching in the bushes in the spot where her father made her promise to stay hidden if anything like this ever happened, Lizzie stared at her father and mother hanging from the tree. Horrified and helpless with no one to turn to, she had no choice but to run away fast and far from the County.

1914

Frank and Olivia crossed the field and came down the path to the big tree. Frank cut the ropes. He laid Lizzie's parents side by side in the snow under the big tree and said a prayer.

Olivia sobbed as they followed Lizzie's footsteps across the snow-covered field.

2014

Doctor McKay chanted.

George was in a trance. Ben walked through the back door into the basement. Dr. Mckay grabbed him. "It's time for the sacrifice."

As the doctor raised the blade to Ben's neck George collapsed, and Ben bolted out of the back door. The doctor dropped the knife and pulled a gun from his waistband.

Detective Bryant descended the basement steps from the kitchen. "Put the gun down, Doc."

"I've waited a long time for this moment," Doctor McKay explained.

Lizzie added, "We all have."

Bryant's gun was trained on the doctor. "But, it's over now."

"You don't have a clue. This is the point where it all ends and begins again." the doctor responded.

Detective Parker had been waiting outside the back door for the signal from Frank. He entered, his gun trained on the doctor, too. Parker warned, "He's right. It's over. You won't get away this time."

"Tell them the secret of the Sons of Suffolk. Tell them how we've lived other lives," George added.

"Oh yes, thanks to Sassie. She kept a record of all the stories right here in this house, but now the veil is rent. The Bureau has the barrette that Olivia gave you for your birthday in

1908, Elizabeth. And Stanley, the photo of your family. Your boy, Ben, was a good boy. And your wife Betsy, a great sacrifice, as well. I miss her too. I hated to kill her, she was such a good worker, and I'm sure a good wife and mother."

Parker realized who the man before him was. "You... you're the one..." Parker held tight to his composure, though he wanted to shoot the man.

"Some things are bigger than us, and when we are called to do them, we must. What a legacy it is to be sacrificed in honor of the book, the vow, and the blade."

"Why don't we let the ladies go?" Parker coaxed.

"The daughters are also bound to the Sons of Suffolk." Dr. McKay explained.

Olivia was confused, "Daughters?"

"Yes, the daughters. Jamie, too." turning to Jamie, "You probably don't remember me. We knew each other a long long long time ago. You cut my dick off!" The doctor continued, "For years, I studied. Coincidence or fate? Our lives. And thanks to Rose..." the doctor said looking at Olivia. "She was your real mother back in 1896. This letter tells the whole story, and after you and Frank left, she eventually remarried, but died, giving birth to your sister, Sassie. Absolutely unbelievable, isn't it?" he asked, laughing. Then, focused on Frank, "And your real Father, the good Reverend, he left a Bible, signed to 'Heather and Franklin, I pray you forgive me one day.' So sad, he was fucking my wife, but that was then, and this is now. And Stanley, tonight you have your daughter back. But, this Ben, he's not your son Ben. But, he is a Ben, nevertheless. A sacrifice for the 1906 County Ball. Isn't that wonderful?"

George collapsed again. The doctor was startled. His gun went off.

George clutched his stomach. He exclaimed, "I was cursed from the start! I never had a chance!"

In the distance, approaching sirens grew louder.

The doctor began to chant again. "It is written. The other five souls are sealed; promised to me during other lifetimes and collected for this night. The prophecy must be fulfilled. The vow must be made whole."

The basement lights began to flicker off and on.

The doctor ran for the door. Lizzie pursued him. She caught the doctor in the darkness between the trees. She knocked the gun out of his hand.

He reclaimed the gun and pointed it at her. Ben sprung from the bushes and lunged for the doctor landing on top of him, and again Dr. McKay lost his grasp of the gun. Lizzie picked it up and aimed it at the doctor.

"Ben, go back to the house."

Ben headed towards an opening in the trees.

Lizzie tossed Dr. McKay's gun into the brush. She moved in closer. The doctor tried to run, but it was too late. He was no match for Lizzie and her blade.

She turned to find Parker and Bryant standing behind her. "He's dead." she said.

Frank reached for her, "Now it's finally over, baby."

Detective Parker asked, "Are you okay? We need to get you out of here."

Agent Connor and his team team approached the scene. Agent Brown asked, "Is your mission complete?"

"Yes," answered Lizzie.

"Well, let's get you out of here and to a doctor right now," added Parker.

Ben, Olivia, and Jamie rushed to Lizzie's side, as she reassured them, "I'm fine. I don't need a doctor. Is George okay?"

"Yes, he's at the hospital. It was just a flesh wound. He'll be fine. I love you, baby, but Parker is right," answered Bryant.

"You're damn right, I'm right! I'm her daddy, and she doesn't have a choice in the matter. Trust me, we're going right now to have a doctor check you out to make sure you and my grandchild are okay!"

2014

Months later, the brightly shining sun warmed the day for a wedding. The sounds of the holy celebration spilled out onto the streets as the wedding party exited the church. Everyone gathered for pictures with the expectant groom and bride as the new family is written into the County registry. Milestones wait to become new memories for the familiar strangers again.

2024

The little girl blew out all 10 candles with one breath. Everyone cheered. There was food, music, and laughter. She was delighted to have the attention of her family and friends focused on her and not her two-year-old brother. She sat on the floor and opened gifts while her family reminisced about her birth nine months after the County Centennial Celebration.

No one ever told her exactly what happened at the Centennial. She learned by listening late at night through the vents in her bedroom and other strategic places in the house. She would sneak and listen to her parents and Granddaddy Stanley talk in codes when he visited.

She heard that five people died, and her mother killed the man who killed the people. She knew her mother was busy with new directives. She didn't know what that meant, but she knew she would find out if she kept listening.

"Can Grandaddy get a kiss from the birthday girl?" Parker asked. She giggled as he kissed her chubby cheek.

He could barely believe how she was growing. For Parker, the last 10 years were filled with joy. A joy that came upon him like an unexpected breeze – refreshing and luxurious. He was happy.

"I am going to live to be 110 years old and have a party every year!" the child proclaimed.

Laughing, Frank added, "Well, honey, that's great. You will be able to take care of your granddad, me, your mom, and your uncle Ben and still have a little time left for yourself!"

Olivia added, "Don't forget about your aunts! You can take care of us too."

They all laughed.

During the party, Lizzie's mind drifted, thinking of what life would be like if her little girl did live to be 110 years old. She imagined what the child could learn, the focus that could be taught, and the work that could be passed on.

Lizzie added, "Let's just enjoy your party now, and we will take it day by day and year by year, sweetheart."

Even with her extrasensory skills and supernatural strength, Lizzie knew that time provided little protection from the pains of life. Yet, each new day would bring another chance to overcome evil.

About the Author:

Crystal Nolen enjoys writing stories, plays, poetry, scripts, and songs. She has performed in various venues from California, Cuba, New York, North Carolina, to Virginia. She has studied at Norfolk State University, the University of Havana, Cuba, the Conservatory for Dramatic Arts in NY, and the school of hard knocks on many of its campuses. She relishes time reading, being with family and friends, and working in the community.

Colophon

Wider Perspectives Publishing regrets to have to announce that the ongoing Colophon page, used to tout artists published in books from WPP, has to be reworked. This is due to the **growing** library of fine writers coming out of, or even into, the Hampton Roads area of Virginia.

Donna Burnett-Robinson
Faith Griffin
Se'Mon-Michelle Rosser
Lisa M. Kendrick
Cassandra IsFree
Nich (Nicholis Williams)
Samantha Geovjian Clarke
Natalie Morison-Uzzle
Gus Woodward II
Patsy Bickerstaff
Edith Blake
Jack Cassada
DezzDaniel Garwood
Jada Hollingsworth
Tabetha Moon House
Travis Hailes- Virgo, thePoet
Nick Marickovich
Grey Hues
Rivers Raye
Madeline Garcia
Chichi Iwuorie
Symay Rhodes
Tanya Cunningham-Jones
    (Scientific Eve)
Terra Leigh
Raymond M. Simmons
Samantha Borders-Shoemaker
Taz Weysweete'
Jade Leonard
Darean Polk
Bobby K.
    (The Poor Man's Poet)

J. Scott Wilson (TEECH!)
Charles Wilson
Gloria Darlene Mann
Neil Spirtas
Jorge Mendez & JT Williams
Sarah Eileen Williams
Stephanie Diana (Noftz)
Shanya – Lady S.
Jason Brown (Drk Mtr)
Ken Sutton
Kailyn Rae Sasso
Crickyt J. Expression
Franzy Civil

Catherine TL Hodges
C. Nolen
Kent Knowlton
Linda Spence-Howard
Maria April C.
Tony Broadway
Zach Crowe

Mark Willoughby
Martina Champion
... and others to come soon.

the Hampton Roads
  Artistic Collective (757
  Perspectives) &
The Poet's Domain
are all WPP literary journals in
cooperation with Scientific Eve or
Live Wire Press

Check for those artists on FaceBook, Instagram, the Virginia Poetry Online channel on YouTube, and other social media.